EGMONT

We bring stories to life

This edition published in Great Britain 2009 by Dean,
an imprint of Egmont UK Limited
239 Kensington High Street, London W8 6SA
All Rights Reserved

Thomas the Tank Engine & Friends™

CREATED BY BRITT ALLCROFT
Based on the Railway Series by the Reverend W Awdry
© 2009 Gullane (Thomas) LLC. A HIT Entertainment company.
Thomas the Tank Engine & Friends and Thomas & Friends are trademarks of Gullane (Thomas) Limited.
Thomas the Tank Engine & Friends and Design is Reg. U.S. Pat. & Tm. Off.

HiT entertainment

ISBN 978 0 6035 6385 0
3 5 7 9 10 8 6 4 2
Printed in Singapore

THOMAS and GORDON
off the Rails

The Rev. W. Awdry
Illustrated by Robin Davies

"Wake up, Gordon," said his Driver one morning. "You've got a special train to pull today."

"Is it coaches or trucks?" asked Gordon.

"Trucks," said his Driver.

"Trucks!" grumbled Gordon. "I won't go. I won't go!"
Gordon began to sulk and his fire wouldn't burn properly.
When Edward pushed him to the turntable, he didn't help at all.

Gordon hissed loudly. "Trucks! I'll show them." And when the turntable was half-way round, he moved slowly forward. He only meant to go far enough to jam the turntable, but once he was moving forward he found he couldn't stop.

"Whoosh," he said, as he went right off the rails, slithered down a bank and landed in a ditch.

The Yard Manager was very cross. "Look what you've done, you silly great engine!" he bellowed. "It will be hours before we can get you out of here."

"Glug," said Gordon, apologetically.

It was dark when the breakdown team came for Gordon.
They brought floodlights and powerful jacks. A crane lifted
Gordon's tender clear and then the workmen attached strong
cables to the back of his cab.

Then the men built a ramp of sleepers and James and Henry,
pulling hard, managed to get Gordon back on to the rails.
"Not such a splendid engine now, are you?" teased a workman.
It was true. Gordon was very wet, very dirty, and he smelt awful!

A few days later, Thomas was at the junction when Gordon arrived with some trucks.
"Pooh!" remarked Thomas to Annie and Clarabel. "Can you smell a smell? A funny, musty sort of smell?"

"No," said Annie and Clarabel. "We can't smell a smell."
"Do you know what I think it is?" said Thomas, staring at Gordon.
"It's ditch water!" But before Gordon could answer, Thomas had
quietly puffed away, giggling to himself.

Later, Thomas took some empty trucks to the mine. Long ago, miners digging for lead had tunnelled into the ground. One of the tunnels went right under the railway line and the ground above was weak.

At a fork in the sidings, a large notice board said, "DANGER. Engines Must Not Pass This Point." Thomas had often tried to get past, but he had never succeeded. Today, though, he had a plan. As his Fireman got out to change the points, Thomas' Driver leaned out of the cab to see where he was going.

"Now!" said Thomas to himself and, bumping the trucks fiercely, he jerked his Driver off the footplate. "Stupid old sign, there's no danger," he said as he followed the trucks past the board. There was a loud rumbling sound and the ground in front of Thomas started to cave in.

"Look out!" shouted Thomas' Driver. The Fireman scrambled into the cab and put Thomas' brakes on. But it was too late. "Fire and smoke!" shouted Thomas. "I'm sinking." And he was. The rails broke and he slid into the pit below.

"Oh dear," Thomas said. "I am a silly engine."
"And a very naughty one, too," said a familiar voice behind him.
"Please get me out, Sir," said Thomas. "I won't be naughty again."
"I'm not so sure," said The Fat Controller. "We can't lift you out with a crane. The ground isn't firm enough. We might have to leave you there for sometime . . . "
"Leave me . . . here?" wailed Thomas.

The Fat Controller thought for a while. "Hmmn," he said,
"I wonder if Gordon could pull you out."
Thomas stumbled out a reply, "G . . . G . . . Gordon?" He wasn't
sure he wanted to see Gordon again just yet.

When Gordon heard about Thomas' accident, he laughed loudly.
"Down a mine is he?" he asked James and Edward.
"How fitting – I always said that he was a minor engine.
Ho-Ho-Ho!" But he hurried to the rescue all the same.

Gordon reached the mine and carefully drew up behind Thomas.

"Poop-poop, little Thomas, have you got that sinking feeling?" he whistled. "We'll have you out of there in a couple of puffs."

Workmen fastened strong cables between the two engines. "Are you ready?" called The Fat Controller. "One, two, three, HEAVE." Very slowly and very carefully, Gordon pulled Thomas back on the rails to safety.

"Thank you for rescuing me," said Thomas to Gordon,
"I was in a bit of a hole!"
His Driver and Fireman checked him over to see where
he was hurt. "I'm sorry I was cheeky."

"That's all right, Thomas," said Gordon. "You made me laugh.
I like that."
Then he whispered carefully, "I'm in disgrace, you know, and it
cheered me up."

Gordon started to tow Thomas back towards Tidmouth Sheds.
"I'm in disgrace, too," said Thomas as they started their journey.
"Why! So you are, Thomas," Gordon replied. "We're both in
disgrace. Shall we form an alliance?"
"An ally – what?" asked Thomas.
"An alliance, Thomas. United we stand, together we fall,"
said Gordon grandly. "You help me and I'll help you."

"Right you are," said Thomas.
"Good! That's settled, then," rumbled Gordon.
And buffer to buffer the allies puffed home.